PUBLIC DEFENDER

Lawyer for the People

by Joan Hewett

photographs by
Richard Hewett

LODESTAR BOOKS
Dutton   New York

Library of Congress Cataloging-in-Publication Data
Hewett, Joan.
  Public defender: lawyer for the people/by Joan Hewett: photographs by Richard Hewett.—1st ed.
    p. cm.
  Includes bibliographical references and index.
  Summary: Text and photographs portray the worklife of a public defender as she investigates
cases and represents poor people in criminal proceedings before the Los Angeles County courts.
  ISBN 0-525-67340-7
  1. Public defenders—California—Los Angeles County—Juvenile literature. 2. Fukai, Janice—
Juvenile literature. [1. Public defenders. 2. Lawyers. 3. Occupations. 4. Fukai, Janice.]
I. Hewett, Richard, ill.   II. Title.
KFC1160.4.Z9H39   1991   90-26389
345.794'9301—dc20   CIP
[347.9493051]   AC

Published in the United States by Lodestar Books, an affiliate of Dutton Children's Books, a
division of Penguin Books USA Inc.
Published simultaneously in Canada by McClelland & Stewart, Toronto
Editor: Rosemary Brosnan   Designer: Barbara Powderly
Printed in Hong Kong   First Edition   10 9 8 7 6 5 4 3 2 1

"If we are to keep our democracy,
there must be one commandment:
Thou shalt not ration Justice."
—Judge Learned Hand, 1953

Janice Fukai is a public defender. She is a lawyer who represents men and women charged with many kinds of crimes. Some are innocent; many are guilty. None has the money to hire a private attorney.

Like bread and butter or camels and the desert, the right to a fair trial and counsel seem to go together. Other than lawyers, few people understand legal terms, procedures, and rules. Innocent people might not be able to establish their defense if they did not know what evidence would be relevant and could be admitted in court—or what evidence would be irrelevant and could not be admitted.

People often assume that free counsel is an age-old American right. The first ten amendments to the Constitution, called the Bill of Rights, took effect in 1791, and the sixth amendment says ". . . the accused shall enjoy the right to a speedy and public trial, by an impartial jury . . . and to have the assistance of counsel for his defense."

During that century, however, no country in the world guaranteed counsel for everyone standing trial, and most American legislators believed the sixth amendment referred only to cases being tried in Federal courts. Some thought it applied to cases in any court if the charge was extremely grave. There were no firm guidelines. Poor people accused of serious crimes received free counsel if and when a judge found it necessary.

Times changed. People began to think about equal justice under the law from a different point of view. Lawmakers argued about the real meaning of the sixth amendment.

In 1931 several poor young men charged with murder were

found guilty in a local court. Because they had not been given counsel until the day the trial started, they had no prepared defense. Outraged at this injustice, some lawyers took the case to the Supreme Court of the United States. In a famous 1932 decision, the Court found that the men had not had a fair trial, and the verdict was overturned.

Other similar cases were brought before the Supreme Court. More often than not, the verdicts were reversed. The Court was clearly saying that under the sixth amendment it did not matter in which court a trial was held—everyone was entitled to a fair trial. But the Court did not find that counsel was needed for a trial to be fair. So free counsel was still, in essence, appointed on a case-by-case basis, when judges found counsel necessary for a fair trial.

In a famous 1963 decision, the Supreme Court said: "... any person haled into court, who is too poor to hire a lawyer, cannot be assured of a fair trial unless counsel is provided for him. ..." Then in 1972 the justices made their meaning even clearer. They said people may not be imprisoned for *any* offense unless they were represented by counsel at their trial.

Today the right of the poor to free counsel is the law of the land. And, in courtrooms across America, a special breed of dedicated lawyers argue their clients' cases. Like Janice Fukai, they are public defenders.

Janice is a Los Angeles County public defender. Although the county office employs some five hundred public defenders, the petite thirty-three-year-old has quickly risen to the top. She now holds the highest rank and represents people charged with felonies—serious crimes. Sometimes she has capital cases and is responsible for defending people who could receive the death penalty.

The old stone downtown criminal court building where Janice works seems like a world unto itself. Security guards flank the outer doors. People crowd the elevators. Public defenders and their assistants have offices on certain floors. District attorneys and their staffs work on others.

Some floors are lined with courtrooms. Defendants—people who have been charged with a crime—along with their wives, husbands, or parents, gather in the corridor waiting for their case to be heard. Lawyers and witnesses also wait. Jurors, wearing identification tags and looking somewhat like tourists, troop through a courtroom door.

A few floors are not listed in the building's directory. The public elevators do not stop there. These are holding floors where defendants are held in cells for several hours till their hearing or trial begins.

Courts are in session throughout the day. Janice has "morning court."

By 7:00 A.M. Janice is getting down to work. She has a cup of coffee and checks her messages. Then, blocking out the sound of fellow workers walking past her office, Janice looks through a case folder. She rereads a police report and reaches for a book to clarify a point.

Public defenders carry heavy case loads; however, they do not work on all of their cases at the same time. Cases go through the courts step by step, hearing by hearing.

Janice often carries thirty or even forty felony cases. Many of her clients are charged with possession of, or selling, illegal drugs. Others are accused of various crimes including assault, burglary, or murder. Janice defends each client until his or her case is settled.

Felony cases start in municipal court with arraignment, where the accused is charged with a crime and answers to it. When the answer, or plea, is not guilty, the case is set for preliminary hearing.

This is almost a mini-trial. The prosecution presents evidence and witnesses, and if the judge decides the government has grounds to support its charge, the case moves to superior court. Then, if superior court hearings do not produce a settlement, the case is set for trial.

This morning Janice will represent five clients in preliminary hearings. In each hearing, she will have the opportunity to cross-examine witnesses and test the strength of the government's case. She will also represent new clients in arraignment court.

"I'm your lawyer. My name is Janice Fukai." Janice speaks to a new client in a lock-up area next to the courtroom where arraignment proceedings will be held. She reads the charge against him out loud and asks questions about what took place.

Then she asks him about his background. "Do you have any prior convictions? What for? Do you have a job?" The answers help Janice guide her client. Found guilty of the same offense, a defendant who seems to be a responsible member of the community will usually get a much lighter sentence than a defendant with a criminal record.

Now Janice talks to her client about elements of the offense, his possible defenses, and the range of sentencing he might expect. Then she pauses and says, "How do you want to plead?"

Shortly after 8:00 A.M. the judge tells the clerk he is ready, and the clerk officially declares, "Arraignment court is now in session." The court reporter, who will record everything that is said, starts taking notes. The bailiff, a law enforcement officer responsible for safe and orderly courtroom proceedings, brings in the first defendant.

Sitting at opposite ends of a long table, Janice and the district attorney face the judge. The district attorney represents the government, and his job is to prosecute the defendant. An accused person is innocent until proven guilty, so the district attorney must prove guilt. The public defender represents and defends the accused.

Each defendant is heard in turn. The charge is read aloud. A translator is present if one of the defendants does not understand English. In a clear voice, the judge questions the defendant to make sure he or she understands the accusation.

Some cases are settled during arraignment. Defendants plead guilty and are sentenced. But most cases continue, and the preliminary hearing date is immediately set.

The judge may order the accused to remain in jail until the hearing. Janice may spring to her feet and present her objections. Her client is young and has no criminal record; imprisonment means contact with hardened criminals. Her client is not a threat to anyone. . . .

H. REID
JUDGE

If Janice is convincing, the judge will ask the accused if he or she promises to return for the hearing. When the defendant says yes, his word is his pledge and he is released. In legal terms, he is released on his own recognizance.

Thousands of criminal cases are brought before the Los Angeles County courts each year. Trials take a long time. If each case ended in trial, the courts would come to a grinding halt. So most are settled in hearings.

Today, four of Janice's preliminary hearing cases are settled, three by plea bargaining. If a defendant starts to waver over his not-guilty plea, plea bargaining is often used. The lawyer for the defense, the district attorney, and the judge agree on a fair sentence. It is probably lighter than the sentence a judge would give if the case proceeded and the accused was found guilty. So the defendant often accepts the terms and pleads guilty.

The judge gives a defendant every chance to change his mind. "Do you know that by pleading guilty you are losing the right to a jury trial? Do you give up that right? Do you know in a trial you have the right to subpoena witnesses (to order witnesses to appear)? Do you understand what it means to give up this right?"

One of Janice's preliminary hearing cases is dismissed because Janice shows that the government does not have enough evidence. The other case will move to superior court.

Janice says, "Our legal system isn't perfect, but it's good. Still, it isn't easy being a public defender. You've got to believe that you're a good person and you're doing the right thing. By and large, people think you should be prosecuting criminals, not defending them. They cannot imagine how you can stand up for 'people like that.'"

Leaning forward, Janice says, "But what would it be like if only some people charged with crimes were entitled to free counsel? Who would have the godlike power to decide who is worth defending and who is not? Public defenders are committed to justice for all. I have never had a client I could not defend. I'm proud of that.

"Some of our clients are simply in the wrong place at the wrong time. They are poor and live in neighborhoods where crime is an everyday activity. Wary police patrol the streets. Now and then they will stop and arrest people without cause. Public defenders keep them from steamrolling over these hapless people. We'll say, 'Why was this person searched or stopped? On what grounds?' "

Day after day, public defenders work under pressure. Lawyers who are not very interested in defending the poor soon leave. After a few years, even dedicated lawyers can burn out.

Janice has been a public defender for eight years and is still going strong. The high-spirited young woman has learned how to pace herself.

When Janice comes home from work, she takes her dog for a jog around the neighborhood. On weekends she gets together with friends at backyard barbecues. And four afternoons a week, in a makeshift gym in the criminal court building, she leads an aerobics class.

Nobody pays for the class or is paid. Any Los Angeles County employee is welcome, and sheriffs, secretaries, court clerks, and district attorneys participate. For Janice, who took a lot of modern dance classes in college, it is a great way of keeping fit and charging up her energy.

Shortly after aerobics, Janice is back at her desk working on a new case. The probation department's report provides her with important basic information: the defendant's known history, the charge, and "elements and relevant circumstances of the offense." Janice often wants additional information, such as her client's medical, welfare, school, and work records. Some agencies are so slow it takes them a month to respond. Janice says, "Getting the information after a hearing is no help. You've got to know how long things take and you've got to move fast."

If an expert can help her client's case, Janice contacts one. Information from ballistic, polygraph (lie detector), and fingerprint experts has enabled Janice to cast doubt on the prosecutor's evidence.

The public defender's office has its own investigators. Janice uses them frequently to dig up important information, but when it comes to checking out the scene of the crime, she likes to take a firsthand look.

Because weekdays are so busy, Janice usually inspects crime scenes on the weekend. Often she will team up with another public defender. They draw a diagram of the site and measure distances. To prove a fact, they might photograph a window or an alleyway. And sometimes Janice may notice something, such as a parking sign or layers of dust on a shattered window, that will back up her client's claim.

The first time Janice sees a client, she may notice something critical. Her eyes fix on his highly discolored black eye. Why doesn't the victim's description of her assailant mention this? Her client plainly had the black eye before the attack because he was apprehended by the police moments later. The evidence will fade, so Janice quickly makes arrangements to have him photographed.

Before each court appearance, Janice sees her clients again. Jails have daytime and evening visiting hours. Inmates and visitors sit in facing cubicles, separated from one another by glass partitions.

Janice tries to get a better idea of what her client is like. Does he or she seem to be telling the truth? Is he or she defiant? Frightened? If a client shifts about in his seat and seems unable to concentrate and answer questions, Janice will ask him if he has a history of mental illness. Although it has not turned up on his records, he may have been in a mental hospital.

When clients repeat their story, they may include additional information. A client charged with first-degree burglary (breaking into a dwelling for criminal purposes) says, "The house was empty; everyone in the neighborhood knew it." Janice reminds her client that the house was furnished. Her client looks amused and says there were a few pieces of broken-down furniture, but the house had been boarded up for years.

Janice's mind races ahead. First-degree burglary carries a stiff penalty because someone breaking into a house might hurt, or even kill, the people who live there. But if a house is unoccupied and the owner has no plan to rent or sell it, the charge might well be second-degree burglary, and that would mean a much shorter sentence. Now she has a lot to check out!

Poor people charged with a crime often wish they had enough money to hire private counsel. Some do not believe that public defenders are even real lawyers. In fact, surveys comparing public defenders and private criminal lawyers show that public defenders rank among the best.

The Los Angeles County public defender system is quite likely the finest of its kind. Founded in 1914, it was the country's first, and it has served as a model for public defender offices across the nation.

If a young lawyer wants to specialize in criminal law, a public defender's office is the place to get first-rate, hands-on training and wide-ranging experience. In turn, public defender systems want capable young lawyers. Los Angeles public defenders go to law schools looking for students with good academic records and an interest in social justice, and they make a special effort to find qualified students with diverse ethnic and cultural backgrounds.

During their first year as Los Angeles County public defenders, lawyers are trained, coached, and supervised by senior public defenders. Then they are assigned to an office and receive their own case load. However, in the true public defender tradition, they are teamed with more experienced court partners. Later they may be assigned to special divisions to broaden their knowledge.

Janice was assigned to the Juvenile Services Division. Because of illnesses and resignations, Janice was immediately given a large number of cases involving serious charges. In short order she grasped the "ins and outs" of juvenile law and gained the attention and respect of her superiors.

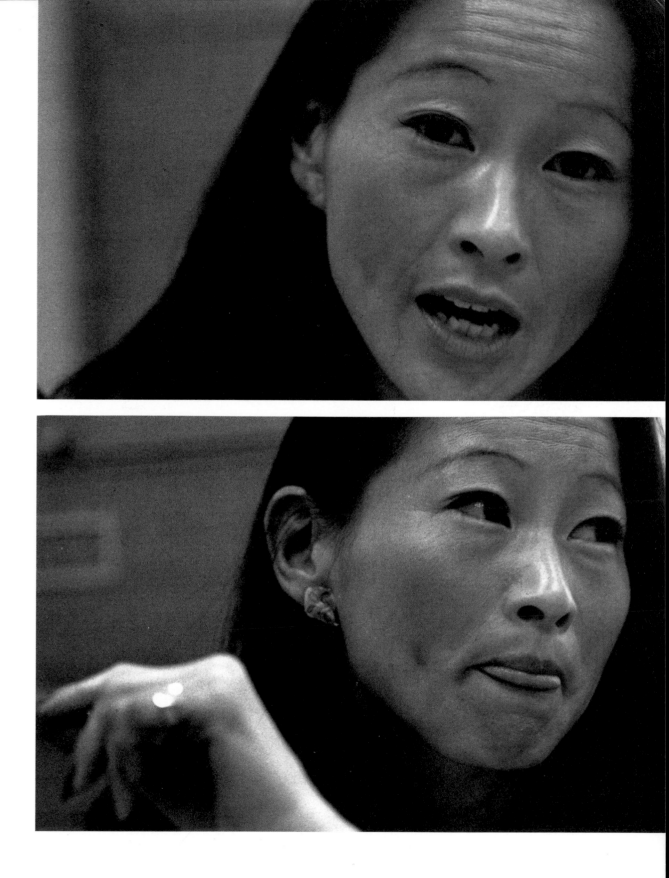

A few years later, after valuable trial experience in other courts, Janice volunteered to train incoming lawyers. Janice produced, directed, and stage-managed hearings so her students could focus on key issues in a "real" setting. And every step of the way, she supervised the cases they were handling.

Within the law offices of the Los Angeles County public defender system, promotion from one rank to another is based on yearly reviews and test scores. A few years ago Janice reached the highest trial-lawyer rank. She smiles and says, "Oh, it was great. I felt so appreciated!"

In the hectic world of criminal law, public defenders are known for their camaraderie. They root for one another, help one another. Janice says, "My court partner has a limited background in felony work, so I give her advice. Someone else will give me advice. At conventions, I get together with public defenders from other areas of the state, and we talk about courtroom techniques and share experiences."

Public defenders care about the men and women they represent. Many clients have led extremely sad lives. By their early thirties, some have a string of convictions for crimes such as assault, burglary, fraud, possession and sale of illegal drugs, and forgery.

Janice says, "That doesn't mean that every twenty-two-year-old who has committed a crime is going to drift into a life of crime. But people usually have a hard time turning their lives around. Alternative sentencing can help them help themselves."

Rehabilitation programs provide counseling, medical help, and job training. First time offenders who plead guilty to nonviolent crimes are prime rehabilitation candidates.

When Janice believes a client can be rehabilitated, she turns to the public defender's alternative sentencing department, and they find the best program or programs for that person. Then, when the case comes up, Janice asks for an alternative sentence and suggests a recommended program. More often than not, the judge agrees.

Janice receives regular reports on each client's progress. After a client completes the one- or two-year program, he or she returns to court. Janice shows the judge that her client has faithfully participated in the program, and the case is dismissed.

Although Janice advises clients to plea-bargain when she thinks it is in their best interest, she never urges. How to plead is a decision only the defendant can make.

"You don't know if your client is innocent," Janice says. "I had a client charged with burglary who had prior burglary convictions and no alibi. The police had fingerprint identification and it seemed like an open-and-shut case." In exchange for a guilty plea, the district attorney offered Janice's client a light sentence. Her client refused to settle. He pleaded innocent and the date of the trial was set.

Janice read up on fingerprints, talked to experts, and discovered there was not total agreement on how closely fingerprints had to match to be identified as the same print.

Each fingerprint has many configurations and is made up of numerous ridges and dots. The sheriff's report identifying Janice's client's fingerprint with the fingerprint lifted from the scene of the crime had been based on a minimal number of matching ridges and dots. In addition, the lifted print was not perfectly clear.

After hearing the evidence, the jury found Janice's client not guilty. Janice says, "I think they were right. As a matter of fact, I think jurors usually are."

Jury selection is an important part of a trial. And the choice of jurors is especially important in credibility cases, when the outcome hinges on who jurors will believe—and witness or witnesses for the prosecution or the defendant.

Janice will be trying a credibility case this week. Her client is a young man charged with selling cocaine. He denies it. According to the arresting officers, they were watching the defendant from a marked car and saw him make the sale.

"It's going to be tough, really tough," Janice said. "People like to believe that police officers do not make mistakes. And no one wants someone trafficking in drugs to go free.

"Still," Janice says, "when ordinary citizens get in that jury box, they take their responsibility very seriously. I've got to pick jurors who have open minds and will truly listen."

Twelve jurors are needed. There is a large, but limited, pool of potential jurors. The first group files into the quiet courtroom. The judge talks to them about being impartial and basing their verdict upon the evidence. He tells them about the case and asks if anyone has a personal interest in the matter. No one answers, and the selection process begins.

Both the prosecutor and the defense may challenge jurors, and each side may refuse to accept a certain number.

Janice tells a juror, "I don't think you are an unfair person, but your police ties concern me. Do you think these ties might make it difficult for you to evaluate an officer's testimony? Do you think it would be easier for you to be fair in another case?"

The woman seems sure she could and would be fair. Janice turns to her client and says in a low voice, "I think she's all right."

Her client replies, "Okay, if you think so . . ."

Questioning another juror, Janice says, "Do you think it is possible for a police officer to exaggerate? Do you think it is possible for a police officer to lie?" The person says yes, but the shocked look that flashes across her face belies her answer. Janice quickly dismisses the juror. Experience has taught Janice to use her eyes and ears and trust her own instincts.

By the middle of the next day, twelve jurors have been sworn in. The prosecutor calls the first witness—one of the arresting officers—to the stand.

The officer's testimony conforms to his original statement. Under cross-examination, Janice brings out that the place of her client's arrest was a known drug hangout. Before the witness steps down, the judge warns him not to talk to anyone about his testimony.

After lunch, while cross-examining the second police officer, Janice repeats something the first officer said. "Did you know he said that?" she asks. The witness says yes. Janice presses the point. "Did he tell you he said that?" The witness hesitates and then says yes. A glance at the jurors tells Janice that their faith in the first officer has been jarred.

Janice uses a "scene-of-the-arrest" diagram when she presents the defense. She shows where her client was standing and where the police were parked. She explains that it was night, it was dark, and there were some two hundred feet between the police and her client. No cocaine was found on her client.

Finally it is time for Janice to sum up, to give her closing argument. Looking thoughtfully at one juror and then another, she says, "Do you carpool? Have you stood on the sidewalk and watched your ride approach, then realized, when the car passed you, that it was a different make and model? You saw what you expected to see.

"Maybe the officers' expectations colored what they saw, and they have made a horrendous mistake. You don't actually have to know why the officers' story might be false. The question is, are you convinced, beyond a reasonable doubt, that they are telling the truth?"

The jurors file out to begin their deliberation, and Janice suddenly feels really tired and overworked. Still, she cannot imagine doing another kind of work. She would hate to be in a big law firm or in a corporation's legal office. She enjoys the challenge of a trial and defending the poor. And oh, how she loves to make a difference!

ACKNOWLEDGMENTS

We are grateful to the public defenders, judges, district attorneys, private attorneys, bailiffs, court clerks, court reporters, translators, legal assistants, courtroom witnesses, and defendants who made this book possible. A special thanks to the Honorable John Reid, Los Angeles Superior Court, and their Honors Rand Schrader and Edward Davenport, Los Angeles Municipal Court, for their kind and invaluable assistance. Thanks also go to Richard Sternfeld, David Carleton, Jordan Yerian, Leona Anderson, Susan Layne, Cameron Bailey, Ursula de Swart, Ann Paul, Don Jim, and Renny Day for their special contributions. And we are particularly indebted to Wilbur F. Littlefield, Public Defender for Los Angeles County, for his confidence in our project and for suggesting public defender Janice Fukai as our subject.

To Janice Fukai, who made this book "come alive," we salute and thank you for your freely given expertise and generous, resourceful, and unflagging cooperation.

GLOSSARY

ACCUSED The defendant in a criminal case.

ASSAULT A willful attempt or threat to inflict injury upon another person.

BALLISTICS The method of gun examination used in criminal cases to find out if a given bullet was fired from a particular gun.

CHARGE Accusation of a crime.

CIRCUMSTANCES Not direct evidence, but facts that indicate the probability or improbability of an event.

CLIENT A person who employs or retains a lawyer to advise and defend him or her in a legal matter.

CLOSING ARGUMENT The final statements by lawyers to a jury, summing up the evidence they have shown and pointing to the evidence the other side has failed to show.

COUNSEL Lawyer, attorney, or counselor; someone who gives advice in a legal matter.

COURT CLERK A person who organizes a judge's daily calendar and keeps a file on all cases the judge hears.

CRIMINAL LAW Laws that define criminal conduct and the punishment to be imposed for such conduct.

CROSS-EXAMINATION Questioning a witness, in a trial or hearing, who has already appeared for and been questioned by the other side.

EVIDENCE In a court case, information or objects presented as proof of a fact.

FRAUD False representation to obtain money or property that belongs to someone else.

GROUND A basis. For example: the ground for a lawsuit, the ground for admitting evidence in a trial.

JURY In a court case, a group of people chosen according to law and sworn to consider the evidence and discover the truth for the purpose of reaching a decision.

JUSTICE (n.) Title given to judges.

JUVENILE LAW A legal system for people under the age of eighteen that is different in some ways from the adult system.

LEGISLATORS People who make laws; members of political organizations such as the Senate, the House of Representatives, and city councils.

OFFENDER A person implicated in carrying out a crime.

PLEA The defendant's reply to a criminal charge.

PLEA BARGAINING A criminal court practice that lets the lawyer for the defense, the prosecutor, and the judge resolve a case by offering the defendant a reduced sentence in return for a guilty plea.

POLYGRAPH A lie detector. A scientific device that records the pulse of a person being questioned. It is believed that dramatic shifts occur when the subject lies.

PROBATION The act of suspending the sentence of a convicted offender for good behavior and giving him or her freedom under the supervision of a probation officer.

PROSECUTE To bring someone to trial to obtain a conviction.

SENTENCE The punishment imposed for committing a crime.

SUBPOENA An order to appear in court on a certain date to give testimony about a particular matter.

TESTIMONY Evidence given by a witness in a hearing or trial while under oath to tell the truth.

TRAFFICKING Illegal trading or dealing in certain goods, such as illegal drugs.

VERDICT The finding of a jury. In criminal cases the verdict must be unanimous.

WITNESS (n.) A person who has observed something; a person who testifies in court to what he or she has seen or heard.

FURTHER READING

Baudry, Jo, and Ketchum, Lynne. *Carla Goes to Court.* New York: Human Sciences Press, 1983. An eight-year-old girl witnesses a crime and testifies about it in court.

Dunnahoo, Terry. *Before the Supreme Court.* Boston: Houghton Mifflin, 1974. The story of Belva Ann Lockwood, a fighter for women's rights, who was the first female lawyer to try a case before the Supreme Court.

Faber, Doris and Harold. *We the People: The Story of the United States Constitution Since 1787.* New York: Charles Scribner's Sons, 1987. Changes in the Constitution and how they came about.

Fincher, Ernest B. *The American Legal System.* New York: Franklin Watts, 1980. Brief history of our legal system, and the roles of lawyers, law enforcement officers, and judges. Discusses differences between adult and juvenile law.

Fincher, Ernest B. *The Bill of Rights.* New York: Franklin Watts, 1978. How American civil rights have evolved. Includes an amendment-by-amendment discussion of the Bill of Rights.

Johnson, Joan. *Justice.* New York: Franklin Watts, 1985. A look at our justice system that concentrates mainly on criminal law.

Kolanda, Jo, and Curley, Patricia. *Trial by Jury.* New York: Franklin Watts, 1987. Jury trials from early times to the present.

Olney, Ross R. and Patricia J. *Up Against the Law: Your Legal Rights as a Minor.* New York: Lodestar Books, 1985. A lively explanation of the rights of people under eighteen.

INDEX

arraignment, 14–20
arrests, 22, 29, 37, 39–42
attornies, private, 4, 32

Bill of Rights, 6
burglary, 14, 30, 35, 37

charges, 4, 6–7, 8, 11, 14, 16, 19,
    22, 26, 37
crimes, 26–29, 30
    capital, 8
    felony, 8, 14, 34, 35, 37
    investigation of, 28–29
    nonviolent, 30, 35
    penalties for, 8, 30
crime scenes, 28, 37
cross-examination, 14, 40

defendants, 11
    financial need of, 4, 6–7, 22, 42
    history and records of, 16, 19, 26,
        30, 35, 37
    imprisonment of, 13, 16, 19, 30
    questioning and examination of,
        16, 19, 20, 21, 30
    release of, 20
    rights of, 6–7, 21, 22
defenses, 4–7, 8, 16, 21, 41
    preparation of, 6, 7, 16, 26–30
dismissal, 21, 36, 39
district attornies, 11, 18, 20, 24, 37
drug trafficking, 14, 35, 37, 40–41

evidence, 6, 21, 38
    discovery of, 28–29, 37
    physical, 28–29, 37
    presentation of, 14, 26, 37

felonies, 8, 14, 34, 35, 37
fingerprints, 26, 37
free counsel, 6–7, 22
Fukai, Janice, 4, 7–8
    daily routine of, 13–26
    public defender career of, 8, 24,
        32–35

guilt:
    of defendants, 4, 7, 16, 20–21
    pleas of, 19, 20–21
    proof of, 18
    verdicts of, 7, 16, 20

imprisonment, 7, 13, 16, 19, 30
innocence, 18
    of defendants, 4, 6
    establishment of, 6, 37
    pleas of, 14, 20, 37
    verdicts of, 37

judges, 18–21, 35–36
    instructions from, 38
    responsibilities of, 14, 19, 20–21
juries, 11, 37–42
    deliberation of, 42
    right to trial by, 6–7, 21
    selection of, 37–39
Juvenile Services Division, 32

law schools, 32
Los Angeles County, 20, 24
    public defender system of, 8, 32–34

mental illness, 30
municipal courts, 14
murder, 6–7, 14

plea bargaining, 20–21, 36, 37
pleas, 16, 36
   change of, 20–21
   guilty, 19, 20–21, 35
   not-guilty, 14, 20, 37
police, 22, 29
   testimony of, 37, 38–42
police reports, 14, 37
polygraphs, 26
preliminary hearings, 13, 14, 19, 20
probation departments, 26
prosecution, 18, 21, 39–40
public defenders:
   assignments of, 7, 32
   belief and commitment of, 21–22, 35
   client's relations with, 16, 19, 22, 29, 30, 35–37
   daily routine of, 14–22
   definition of, 4
   heavy case loads of, 14, 32
   history of, 6–7
   information gathering of, 16, 26, 28–30, 37
   private attornies and, 32
   ranking and promotion of, 8, 34
   responsibilities of, 8, 18, 20, 21, 22, 26–30
   stress common to, 22, 42

public defenders (continued)
   training and experience of, 32–34

rehabilitation programs, 35–36

sentences:
   alternative, 35–36
   determination of, 16, 20, 35
   guilty pleas and, 19, 20–21, 35
   light, 16, 20, 30, 37
settlements, 14, 19, 20–21
sixth amendment, 6–7
subpoenas, 21
Supreme Court, U.S., 7

testimony, 37, 38–40
trials:
   cases proceeding to, 19, 20
   jury, 6, 21, 37–42
   murder, 6–7

verdicts, 7, 16, 20, 37, 38

witnesses, 11
   cross-examination of, 14, 40
   defense, 37
   expert, 26, 37
   prosecution, 14, 37, 39–42
   subpoena of, 20